# The Boy and the Dragon

**Francis Gordon Clark**

## Illustrations by Jane Swan

*Dedicated to Xavi, Julia, Honor, Frank and Louis.*

First published in Great Britain in 2005. Copyright © 2005 Francis Gordon Clark

**British Library Cataloguing-in-Publication Data**
A CIP record for this title is available from the British Library

ISBN 1 84114 421 5

**HALSGROVE**
Halsgrove House, Lower Moor Way, Tiverton, Devon EX16 6SS
Tel: 01884 243242   Fax: 01884 243325
email: sales@halsgrove.com   website: www.halsgrove.com

Printed and bound by D'Auria Industrie Grafiche Spa, Italy

nce upon a time a wonderful boy was born.

He was a very lucky boy because he had a lovely Mummy and a lovely Daddy and a lovely sister. They all lived together in a beautiful house with a big garden far, far away in a very hot country called Singapore.

In the garden there were all sorts of exciting things to do and special things to play with and the boy was very happy.

One day, when he was about six years old, the boy was playing in his garden when a Dragon flew down from the sky and perched beside a tree where the boy had a house that had been built for him by his Daddy.

"Don't be frightened," said the Dragon. "I have been chosen by the Head Dragon to be your Mentor and I have come to have a look at you. How do you do?"

"How do you do," said the boy who was very surprised by his visitor. He had seen Dragons sometimes in the streets and sometimes he had thought he had seen them flying high in the sky and had tried to catch them but he had never seen one so close before.

It was beautiful; coloured red and gold it had shiny scales, big claws, a huge tail and silvery wings.

"What is a Mentor?" asked the boy.

The Dragon cleared his throat and a great burst of flame came out of his mouth and whooshed over the boy's head. "Well," he said, "I will explain. You live in a very nice house, do you not?"

"Yes," said the boy.

"And you always have enough to eat, and you have a lot of beautiful toys like the jeep I see over there, and you do exciting and interesting things like diving and skiing and travelling to lots of different places, do you not?"

"Yes," said the boy.

"And you go to a very good school where the teachers are both kind and intelligent and make sure that you learn your lessons really well. And those teachers say that you are one of the brightest and cleverest people in your class. Is that not right?"

"Yes," said the boy.

"And you have a Mummy and Daddy who love you and look after you all the time, do you not?"

"Yes," said the boy.

"So," said the Dragon, "you must see that you are one of the luckiest boys in the whole world.

"Now we Dragons are the keepers of good luck and when we find someone who has been born with lots of it we send one of our Dragons along to make sure that he is using it properly and that Dragon becomes the boy's Mentor."

"How do I use my luck properly?"

"By not wasting it. If you have nice toys you look after them. If you have enough food you eat it. If you are asked to do something by the people who love you or by the teachers in your school you do it. And you are kind to other people, particularly to those who are not as lucky as you.

"If you do these things the luck stays with you as you get older and you are able to do more and more exciting things.

"If you want to be a helicopter pilot for instance you must pass your flying exams. You can only pass exams if you have learned your lessons in school.

"You can only be a great leader of men like
a general in the army or the prime minister
of a country if you can make people like
and trust you.

"You can only be a secret agent if you
have done special training and learned
how to deal with baddies.

"If you want one day to have a beautiful wife
and lovely children you must be able to look after them.

"You learn that all these things come from your
Mummy and Daddy, from your school and from
all the other people around you who love you.

"Good luck is very rare and there is not enough to
go round everybody.  So if we find someone who
is wasting it we take it away from him and give it
to someone else.  But before that happens we
always give the person a warning."

"What happens if I don't look after my luck properly and you take it away?" asked the boy.

"You would find things starting to go wrong.  It would be small things at first. Your toys might breakdown or even disappear.

"You would not do so well at school perhaps. Your teachers would stop trying to help you because you were not trying at your lessons any more.

"You might get ill because you were not eating properly. The illness might make you weak so that you could not play the games and sports that you enjoy.

"Your Mummy and Daddy would become very sad and you would not have such happy times with them and that would be a terrible thing to happen.

"Of course with nearly all our boys and girls everything is fine because they know they are lucky and they want to keep things that way.

"After all it would be very silly for someone to throw his chances away and I am sure that you are much too clever to do that. Just you remember what I have told you.

"And now it is time for me to be going. Goodbye."

The Dragon gave the boy a friendly smile and spread his silver wings and flew off.

"Goodbye," said the boy.

Just then his Mummy came out of the house and asked him to whom he was talking.

"The Dragon," he said.

"I didn't see a Dragon," said Mummy.

"That's because he can be invisible. But he is my Mentor and I can see him when he wants me to."

✦

For a few days the boy was very excited by what the Dragon had said to him. He played with his toys in his lovely house and garden and he enjoyed his school and tried really hard with his lessons.

He ate all his food.

He did what his Mummy and Daddy asked him to do because he knew that they were very wise and that they loved him very much.

He was very happy and he laughed and played with his sister and with his friends and everyone was happy to be with him.

But the days passed and the Dragon did not come back and slowly the boy began to forget about him.

He forgot that he had a Mentor.

He forgot that he was one of the most special boys in the world and he forgot about his luck.

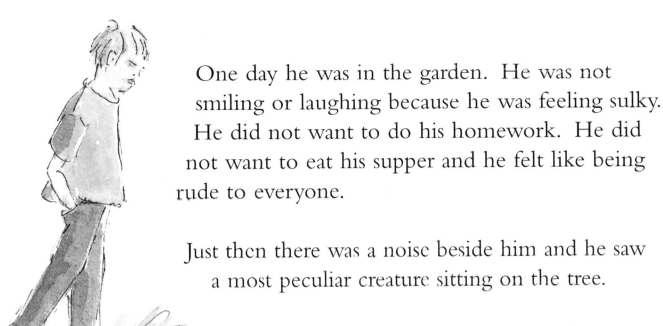

One day he was in the garden. He was not smiling or laughing because he was feeling sulky. He did not want to do his homework. He did not want to eat his supper and he felt like being rude to everyone.

Just then there was a noise beside him and he saw a most peculiar creature sitting on the tree.

It was a bit like a black sausage with short legs and a head like a snake. It had small piggy eyes that were looking hard into the boy's.

"Hello," it said in a rather oily voice.

"Hello," said the boy. "Who are you?"

"I am Nogard and I have come to help you."

"How can you do that?" asked the boy.

"Well," said Nogard, "I know that right now you
are feeling pretty fed up with everything.

"You don't want to do your homework. You don't want
to eat your meals and you don't want to go to bed when
you are told to. Is that right?"

"Yes," said the boy, "I am really bored and angry with people."

"No problem. I am your Rotnem and I know what the
matter is. You are not letting yourself do what you want to do.

"If you don't feel like going to bed for instance, just hide.

"If you don't want to eat, just leave the food on the plate and run off. It could not be easier and you would feel much better because you would be in control."

The boy thought about this and the idea of him doing just what he wanted seemed like fun.

"What's a Rotnem?" he asked.

"We Rotnems believe that everybody should do exactly what they want and not be bossed about by their schoolteachers or their parents. That is the way to be happy. You give it a try."

"But if I don't do what my teachers tell me or if I am rude to my Mummy and Daddy they will be angry with me."

"Well you just be angry back and they will soon let you have what you want. After all there is nothing that they can really do and you will feel tremendous. I shall be around although you won't see me all the time and I will watch how you are getting on.

"I am going to make you a member of our tribe and give you a special name.  I shall call you Ogini."

The boy did not think it was a very nice name but he was pleased to have been made a member of the tribe and so he said nothing.

The next day at breakfast time the boy did not eat his food. When his Mummy tried to make him he said, "I don't want to eat it and you cannot make me because I am a member of a special tribe and my name is Ogini."

His Mummy thought this was very strange and told his Daddy that something bad had happened.

His Daddy spoke to the boy but he refused to listen.

During the next few days the boy behaved very badly indeed.

He did not eat his food.  He did not do his homework.
He ran away and hid when it was time for him to go to bed.
When he was found he shouted at his Mummy and when
she shut him in his room he tried to break down the door.

He did not get ready to go to school in the morning and
was naughty in the car all the way there.

But in spite of all his bad behaviour and not doing what
he was told, the boy did not feel any happier.  He was always
arguing with his Mummy and she no longer looked happy
and smiling.

But whenever he wondered whether something was wrong
Nogard would appear beside him and tell him that he was
doing splendidly.

One day Nogard said that he was going to make Ogini one of the leaders in the tribe and Ogini thought that sounded really grand.

He went into the garden next door and told his friend that he was going to be a tribe leader.

"It cannot be a very nice tribe if you are going to be one of its leaders because you have changed. You used to be good fun to play with but now you get rough and angry sometimes and I do not like being with you as much as I used to," said his friend.

This made the boy rather worried so he went back into his own garden and decided to play with his jeep.

It was a beautiful jeep for which his Daddy had made
a special roof so that you did not get wet when it rained.

But … the jeep was not there!

He looked everywhere but it was nowhere to be found.

He rushed into the house shouting, "My jeep has gone.
What have you done with it?  I want it back now."

His Mummy came out and said that she had not touched
the jeep and that she had no idea where it could be.  It could
hardly have been stolen because the gates were kept shut all
the time so its disappearance was a great mystery.

When his Daddy came home that evening the boy rushed
up to him crying and told him that his jeep had gone.

His Daddy was very worried and talked to his Mummy about
it but neither of them could think of what had happened to it.

The boy was very unhappy because the jeep was his
best toy.  He went to bed that night feeling rather
sick and a bit frightened.

The next day he was not feeling at all well. He went into the garden but the jeep was still not there.

He had a tummy-ache and a headache and he had a temperature and he did not want his food.

Suddenly there was a whoosh and there was the Dragon sitting by the tree beside him.

"O Dragon," said the boy, "please help me. My jeep has disappeared and no one knows where it is."

The Dragon was not smiling.

"I have been watching your behaviour since we met and I have been extremely upset by what I have seen. You have been wasting your luck and that is why your jeep has gone. Your health will begin to suffer too. How are you feeling by the way?"

"Not very well," replied the boy and he burst into tears as he thought of all the things that he had done since he met the Dragon.

"I think you had better tell me everything that has happened since I came and saw you," said the Dragon.

"Everything was fine to begin with. Then one day I was in the garden feeling a bit bored, when Nogard arrived and told me how I could be happy. He said my name was Ogini and that he was a Rotnem and that I could become an important member of his tribe if I just did what I wanted. Every time I was unhappy he appeared and said I was doing really well and if I went on I could be a tribe leader."

The Dragon was still not smiling. In fact he was absolutely furious.

"So," he said, "you forgot what I told you about your being one of the luckiest boys in the whole world.

"Now listen to me. That black thing called Nogard is all bad. The Nogards hate people who are good and who try to make the world a better place. They are in fact the opposite of Dragons and that is why they are Dragon spelt backwards.

"They always try to make children waste all their good luck so they won't be able to grow up into happy, useful people. They call themselves Rotnems because that is Mentor spelt backwards and it is the Mentors' work they are trying to destroy.

"And they give their victims nasty names that are the reverse of really nice ones. What is the reverse of Ogini for example?"

The boy thought for a moment. "Inigo!" he said with a huge grin.

"Right on," said the Dragon, "that's a much nicer name don't you think?

"Now if you remember I told you that we always gave people a warning before their luck started to be taken away, so if you look over there you will see that the jeep is back in its usual place.

"And if I am not much mistaken you are no longer feeling sick but are looking forward to your tea, which you will eat with no fuss and great pleasure. Am I right?"

"Yes," said Inigo with another huge grin.

"Good," said the Dragon, "there is just one more thing to be done." He closed his big Dragon eyes and switched on his magic orbs so that he could see even the things, which were invisible. Then as quick as lightening he shot into the air and was back in a flash with Nogard in his claw.

"So you thought you were going to be a Rotnem to my boy, did you?

"You thought you were going to turn him into a no-good Nogard, did you?

"Let me tell you, if we put a Mentor onto someone we don't stand any nonsense from anyone.

Goodbye Nogard. You are history." A big burst of flame roared out of the Dragon's mouth and Nogard completely disappeared.

"Well that's that," said the Dragon, "but remember things have not changed. You will soon be seven with another year of new things to learn and new things to enjoy.

"Remember that you have had a warning. That was the age six warning and it was not too serious and you got back the jeep and you recovered your health.

"As you get older and more able to stand up for yourself the warnings get bigger and sometimes things don't come back, so no more warnings please."

Inigo was so happy to see his jeep again and so glad that he was feeling better that he ran into the house shouting "Mummy, Mummy, Mummy, the jeep has come back and I am feeling well again and I am never going to be cross and naughty ever again and its all because I have had a warning and the Dragon has blown away the Nogard and my name is Inigo not Ogini and everything is all right again."

His Mummy wondered what Nogard and Ogini was all about but she was much too wise to ask and anyway she was just so happy that Inigo was his lovely self once more. So she gave him a big kiss and said what a marvellous Dragon he must be.

"I am going out to thank him," said Inigo and he rushed back into the garden.

"Good O," said the Dragon. "Before I go I am going to give you a reminder ride."

"What's a reminder ride?"

"Jump on my back and I will show you."

Inigo climbed onto the Dragon's back where he found a comfortable place to sit. The Dragon arranged his scales round the boy so that he was quite safe and with a flap of his silvery wings soared into the air.

Up they went until they saw a rainbow in the sky ahead of them and over the arch was written **DRAGON LAND** in big letters.

They swooshed through the gate and there were lots of other Dragons there. They waved at Inigo and his Dragon and said, "Welcome to Dragon Land."

Inigo waved back. He could hardly believe that was seeing so many beautiful creatures all together.

They flew on until they came to a big cloud with a lovely silver lining. There was a door into it on which was written **Head Dragon's Lair**.

Beside the door was a round hole with a notice that said "Flame here." The Dragon blew a short burst of flame into the hole and there was a rumble of thunder from inside.

"Who is there?" said a deep voice.

"Mentor number one," said the Dragon. "I have come to ask permission to give Inigo a reminder ride."

Out of the door came the Grandfather of all Dragons. He was magnificent. He was even bigger than the Mentor. His scales were pure gold and they shimmered in the sun more brightly

than anything Inigo had ever seen. He looked at Inigo with
his enormous green eyes and asked the Mentor if his boy had
been good.

"We had a few age six problems but he is a good lad and I am not expecting any more trouble."

"Harrumph," said the Head Dragon and a huge blast of fire shot out of his mouth and into the distance where it became a shooting star. "I should think not indeed. I have looked up his form and he is quite one of the luckiest ones we have got. Right, permission granted but no more backsliding, Inigo. Understand?"

"Yes sir," said Inigo.

"Off you go then. Remember I expect a lot from you. Good luck."

There was another harrumph and another shooting star and the Head Dragon went back into his lair saying he was very busy getting ready for the Chinese New Year.

"**S**it tight," said the Dragon and off they went. Presently they came to a signpost cloud and on it was written: Inigo August 8th 1997, with an arrow pointing downwards and there below Inigo saw all the people whom he had ever known.

INIGO AUGUST 8th 1997

First they flew over Singapore and he saw all his friends and all his family. He waved to them but because he was on the Dragon's back he was invisible just like the Dragon himself and they could not see him.

But they must have felt that something good was happening because they all looked up and laughed happily as he went by.

He saw his first school where he learnt about colours and reading and writing and he saw his French school where he was now and he thought about what the Dragon had said about learning things.

They flew over the sea to England and looking down Inigo could see the house where he stayed.
It had a big garden and there were tractors to ride on and a field with a big bull called Ginger Nuts and lots of cows.

They flew on and he saw another house with a lake and horses standing by. And he saw yet another place where he had slept in a tent with lots of his cousins.

They left England and he
was looking down on a huge
brown land surrounded by
golden sand and sparkling
blue water and the Dragon
told him that it was called
Australia.  Inigo remembered
how they had swum in the sea
and played in the garden and
how he had been given a bicycle
for Christmas.

Suddenly he saw a very tall tower and
he realised that they were now over
Paris and there right below them
was the Tour Eiffel, which he had
climbed up only a short time ago.
It was in Paris that he met the
waiter who had told him he
spoke French so well.

Then they were over huge
mountains covered in
brilliant white snow,
which they never saw in
Singapore, and there they
all were skiing together.

Then they were back in
Singapore and he saw himself
going in the boat with his Daddy and
Mummy and his sister Honor and he saw himself diving with
a real air tank among amazing fishes.

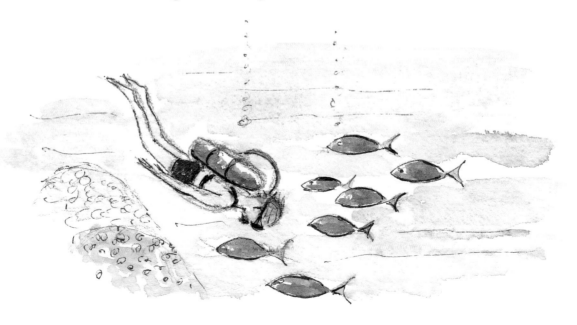

"There you are," said the Dragon, "That is just about the best and most exciting life I have ever seen one of my boys have. Just look behind you. And see all that luck."

Inigo turned and there laid out below were all the beautiful places and all the wonderful people that he had just seen. His whole life past was stretched out behind him and beside each different part of it was a shiny piece of gold.

He turned back again. Ahead of them the sky
was as black as the darkest night and set in it were
the most beautiful stars Inigo had ever seen.

"What is in there?" he asked.

"That is the land of the future," said the Dragon. "In there is what is going to happen next. Not even the Head Dragon can go there.

"You see the stars in the cloud ahead. Each star is a piece of good luck. If you look after your luck each year a star will come out of the cloud and there will be more shiny pieces for you to look back on.

"The important thing to remember is that while you cannot do anything about the future you can do lots about the present. And the better you do now the better the next bit is likely to be.

"Now it is long past your bedtime so it is time for me to take you home."

Down they went faster than a swooping hawk and Inigo found himself back on the ground.

"I shall not say not good-bye but au revoir. After all you speak French and I shall certainly see you again.
I won't give you a kiss.
We Dragons find kissing difficult. We are apt to give people nasty burns."

"Au revoir Dragon. Come and see me again when I have collected a few more stars," said Inigo giving the Dragon a big hug.

There was a soft whoosh and Inigo was back in his bed dreaming of all the things that had been and all the things that might be.

And that would be another story.

✻